# Look Out Kindergarten, Here I Come!

## by Nancy Carlson

SCHOLASTIC INC.

New York  Toronto  London  Auckland  Sydney
Mexico City  New Delhi  Hong Kong

ISBN 0-439-21253-7

Copyright © 1999 by Nancy Carlson.
All rights reserved.
Published by Scholastic Inc., 555 Broadway, New York, NY 10012,
by arrangement with Viking Children's Books, a division of Penguin Putnam Inc.
SCHOLASTIC and associated logos are trademarks and/or registered
trademarks of Scholastic Inc.

12                                                          4  5  6/0

Printed in the U.S.A.                    24

First Scholastic printing, September 2001

Set in Avenir

To Maureen Beck—a dedicated educator who helped me come up with the idea for this book

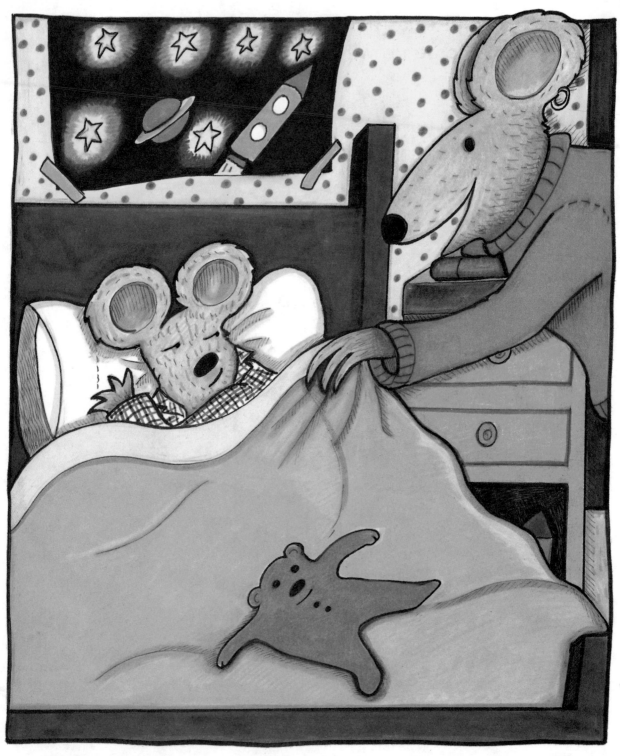

"Wake up, dear," said Henry's mom. "It's the first day of kindergarten."

"Oh boy! Let's go!" said Henry. He had been
getting ready for this day all year.
"Not so fast," said his mom. "First you need to
wash up and get dressed."

So Henry brushed his teeth the way his dentist had shown him and washed behind his ears.

Then he buttoned his shirt and snapped his jeans and *almost* tied his shoes.

"Okay, I'm all ready for kindergarten!" said Henry.
"Not so fast," said his mom. "First you need a
good breakfast."

So Henry ate three  pancakes and a bowl
of fruit and drank a big glass of milk.

"Now I'm ready to go!" said Henry.
"Not so fast," said his mom. "You still need to pack up your supplies."

So Henry packed pencils, scissors, crayons, paper, glue, an apple, and . . .

a photo of his mom and dad
(in case he got lonely).

"Now I'm ready!"
said Henry.

"What do you think we'll do first?" asked Henry.
"Do you think we'll paint?"

"Sure you will," said his mom. "Just like at home."
"Good!" said Henry. "What else will we do?"

"You'll probably learn your ABCs," said his mom.

"Hey, I already know the letters in my name!" said
Henry. "What will we do after that?"

"You'll sing songs,

and play games,

and you might practice counting," said his mom.

"One, two, three flowers," said Henry. "I can count to ten, because we practiced counting with buttons. What comes next?"

"You'll make fun things in arts and crafts, and you'll read stories."

"But I can't read!" said Henry.
"That's okay," said his mom. "You'll start by listening. Reading comes later."

"Here we are," said Henry's mom.
"It's so *big*," said Henry. "What if I get lost?"

"Remember, we found your room and your cubby at Kindergarten Roundup," said his mom. "But you can always ask a teacher for help."

When Henry got to his room and
saw lots of new faces, he said,

"I want to go home!"

"Why don't you come in and look around?" said
his teacher, Ms. Bradley.

So Henry looked around. He saw the art corner.
He saw letters and numbers that he knew.

He saw a bookcase full of books, and he met a new friend to play with.

"Well, what do you think?" asked Henry's mom.
"I think I might stay for a while, Mom," said Henry,

"because kindergarten is going to be fun!"